Space Invaders

READ ALL THE SHARK SCHOOL BOOKS!

SHARK SCHOOL

#10 Space Invaders

BY DAVY OCEAN
ILLUSTRATED BY AARON BLECHA

ALADDIN New York London Toronto Sydney New Delhi

WITH THANKS TO PAUL EBBS

ALADDIN

An imprint of Simon & Schuster Children's Publishing Division
1230 Avenue of the Americas, New York, NY 10020
First Aladdin hardcover edition March 2019
Text copyright © 2019 by Hothouse Fiction
Illustrations copyright © 2019 by Aaron Blecha
Also available in an Aladdin paperback edition.
All rights reserved, including the right of reproduction in whole or in part in any form.
ALADDIN and related logo are registered trademarks of Simon & Schuster, Inc.
For information about special discounts for bulk purchases, please contact
Simon & Schuster Special Sales at 1-866-506-1949 or business@simonandschuster.com.
The Simon & Schuster Speakers Bureau can bring authors to your live event. For more
information or to book an event contact the Simon & Schuster Speakers Bureau at 1-866-248-3049
or visit our website at www.simonspeakers.com.
Series designed by Karin Paprocki
Jacket designed by Nina Simoneaux
Interior designed by Mike Rosamilia
The text of this book was set in Write Demibd.
Manufactured in the United States of America 0219 FFG
2 4 6 8 10 9 7 5 3 1
Library of Congress Control Number 2018953531
ISBN 978-1-4814-6556-4 (hc)
ISBN 978-1-4814-6555-7 (pbk)
ISBN 978-1-4814-6557-1 (eBook)

Space Invaders

CHAPTER 1

"FIVE!!!!!!!!!!!!!!!!!!!!!!" I yell as I blast out of my bedroom at top speed.

"FOUR!!!!!!!!!!!!!!!!!!!!!!!!!!!!!!!!!!!" I shout as I zoom down the stairs.

"THREE!!!" I scream as I hook my hammer head on the corner of the kitchen door so it will

swing me around into the kitchen in an awesome double-tail-swirl.

"TWO!!" I roar as I smash through the currents and shatter the quiet of my parents' breakfast.

"ONE!!!" I holler as my fin skids perfectly across the surface of the table, scattering plates and cups in every direction!

"TOUCHDOWN!" I howl at the top of my gills as I thump into my chair, grabbing a spinning spoon.

"Major Hammer to Fishon Control," I say, flipping the box of Kelp Krispies over my floating bowl. "We have achieved splashup!!!!"

My dad, Hugo Hammer, the mayor of Shark Point, looks at me angrily.

My mom, Harriet Hammer, looks at me, and she's not smiling.

"Harry!" they both shout. "What on ocean are you doing?"

"I'm a terranaut!" I shout back, making roaring rocket noises. I leap off my chair and fall to the floor, pretending I'm struggling against the increased gravity of land!

In your leggy airbreather world you have spacetronauts and astrowomen or whatever. Leggy airbreathers who go into space and land on the moon, or fly to the International Space Station and do experiments.

Under the sea we have terranauts ("terra" means "land") and send rockets up to land so we can explore and stuff.

4

Right this second I'm cosmically excited, because the lead terranaut, Buzz Sharkfin, is coming to visit our school! And we are going to take turns giving him presentations about what terra exploration means to us.

TODAY!!!

I've never met the ocean's greatest terranaut before, but I do have all Buzz Sharkfin's shows. In fact, if I just flick my tail onto the remote control, I can get one playing right now on the flat-screen.

"I was watching that!" says Mom as the picture changes to a slow-motion picture of Buzz Sharkfin in his water-filled protective terrasuit, climbing out of his terraship.

I watch with openmouthed wonder as Buzz pushes his lead fin into the sand to make the first sharkprint on land, saying, "That's one small paddle for shark, but one giant superswim for shark-kind!"

"Turn it back to your mom's program, Harry," says Dad.

"Oh, come on, Dad, let me watch this. It's amazing."

"How many times have you watched it?" Dad asks.

"Ummmmmmmm . . . ," I stall.

"How many?"

"Four thousand, six hundred, and twenty-three," I say, looking down and feeling my cheeks turning red. "Since last Wednesday."

"Exactly," says Dad. "Now turn it back." Ummmmmm . . .

Oh no! But suddenly there was a TER-RIBLE ACCIDENT! I pressed the wrong button on the remote control!

The show reran to the moment Buzz said, "That's one small paddle for shark, but one giant superswim for shark-kind," and I had the *awful* job of watching him make that historic finprint again.

Mom and Dad are not happy.

Oops!

I glance at the kitchen clock. Normally I wouldn't be leaving for school for another fifteen minutes or so—certainly not before my friends Ralph the Pilot Fish, Joe the Jellyfish, or Tony the Tiger Shark get here—but not today. Checking for about the millionth time to make sure my presentation for Buzz is in my backpack, I *swoosh* past Mom and Dad and race for the door.

Mom and Dad are calling to me, but I'm zooming too fast to hear them—today, nothing is going to stop me getting to school first!!!

Except everyone got there before me.

Here's a list of everything that's going on outside school when I arrive—and none of it makes me happy.

1. Tony has his nose pressed up against the school gates, trying to keep his place as the other kids and squids crowd around him.

2. Ralph is hanging on to Tony's tail for dear life as the crowd pushes forward.

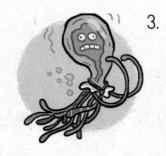

3. Joe is right at the back saying, "Perhaps Buzz isn't coming and we can all just get on with a normal, safe, nonscary day. Please?"

HA
HA
HA

4. And Rick . . . Yeah, Rick the Reef Shark, my number one least favorite kid in school because . . . This needs a Rick sublist:

He always creeps up behind me and FLUBBERS my goofy hammery head when I least expect it.

He's also the one who wants to be the best out of everyone in class. Even MORE

THAN I DO!!!! And this needs a Rick sub-sublist because it's so bad!!!

He's … He's … RICK'S SHOVING HIS WAY TO THE FRONT OF THE CROWD, PUSHING KIDS AND SQUIDS OUT OF THE WAY, WEARING A BRAND-NEW BUZZ SHARKFIN OFFICIAL BRAND T-SHIRT AND CARRYING AN AUTHENTIC BUZZ SHARKFIN BACKPACK.

The kids and squids are getting out of his way as if Rick *is* Buzz Sharkfin!

Rick swims along with a grin so wide it might meet around the back of his head and make his nose drop off.

I wish.

"Everyone move back please! I need to open the gates!" announces Mrs. Shelby, our teacher. She's waving her flipper around and pushing the hard edge of her turtle shell against the gates so they can swing open.

The crowd swims backward in the water, leaving Rick alone there like the gates had opened just for him!

Rick does a tail-endy and a half-barrel into a bow, then shouts, "Hey, Rubberhead!" at me.

Then suddenly . . .

WHAAAAAAAAAAAAAAAAAAAM!!!!!

"ARRRRRRRRRRRRRRRRGHH!!!!!!!!!!!!!!!"

"SCREAMMMMMMMMMMMMMMM!!!!!"

"Heeeeeeeeeelllllp!!!!!!!!!!!!!!!!!!!!!!!!"

A massive green shellicopter descends
from the waves above—its blades spinning

13

wildly and its engines roaring like a hundred storms.

Rick is caught in the swirling wake, picked up and sent flying off into the water, up and up, and away over the school!

By the time the shellicopter lands, the door opens and the ocean's greatest terranaut climbs out, and Rick, I'm glad to report, is nowhere in sight!

CHAPTER 2

"FIVE!!!!!!!!!!!!!!!!!!!!!!!!!"

The whole class cheers as Buzz Sharkfin floats through the school gates, waving a mighty fin as he goes.

"FOUR!!!"

We yell as we look at his gleaming teeth, his awesome hair, and his tanned face.

BUZZ SHARKFIN

"THREE!!!"

We howl as Buzz gives a little bow to Mrs. Shelby, and her face turns pinker than rose coral.

"TWO!!!"

We roar as Buzz turns to wave near the school door, and his shellicopter takes off into the wide blue yonder!

"ONE!!!"

We scream as Buzz disappears inside to prepare for his speech to us about his adventures as a terranaut!!!!!

"OI!!!!!!!!!!!!!!! RUBBERFACE!!!!!!!!!!!!!!!!!!!!!!!"

Rick bellows in my ear as he appears next to me, once again flubbering my hammer head.

"Look at me!" Rick grabs my still twanging hammer and puts his face right up close to mine. I can smell the rotten waft of sea cow yogurt on his breath. "Why didn't you tell me Buzz's shellicopter was landing behind me? I wound up in the garbage cans on the other side of the school!"

Rick picks a lump of three-day-old crab-egg-scramble out of his ear and swims into the school, leaving a stinky cloud of garbage juice in his wake. "You're in real trouble now, Rubberface!" he calls back to me.

Oh great.

Everything is my fault.

Again.

"Terra exploration isn't just glamour and giving talks to crowds of schoolkids," Buzz Sharkfin says as he floats on the stage set up in the gym. "Although there is quite a bit of that."

"No," Buzz continues, "being a terranaut is a dangerous, but above all, incredible job to have."

"See?" whispers Joe in my ear. "He said it's 'dangerous' *first*. Not last or in the middle, but first! Doesn't he know that my nightmares are already having nightmares of their own?!?!"

As if to underline how nervous Joe is, his bottom toots with fear, not once, not twice, but ten times!

Buzz continues.

"I may have been the first shark to successfully make a finprint on the surface of the land, but our journey as

oceankind must not end there. There must be further missions, there must be further exploration, and you schoolkids are the future terranauts. You are the brave . . ."

"I'm not," whispers Joe.

I shush Joe as I see Rick scowling at us.

Buzz goes on. "Sadly, I can't be a terranaut forever. One day I'll make my last flight, and after that, it'll be up to kids like you to replace me."

I feel my heart swelling in my chest. Just the thought of it—riding a roaring rocket to the top of the ocean, out into the atmosphere—to touch down on another world. The land!

"Which is why I will now be joined onstage by Dr. Lillian Lamprey, from NASA—The National Aqua-Terranautical and SeaSpace Administration—to talk to you about my next mission . . . and how one of you might get to play a part!"

My heart pounds as Buzz floats back to let Dr. Lamprey, who is wearing a white coat with lots of pen-fish sticking out of the top pocket, swim up onto the stage. What did Buzz mean, one of us might get to play a part?!

"Today," Dr. Lamprey begins, pushing

her glasses back over her top lip with a flick of a tail, "NASA is announcing that the next mission for Buzz Sharkfin will be a journey farther onto terra than we have ever attempted before! We are building a rocket so powerful that it will carry him, higher and faster, up over the mountains that surround Shark Point, deep into the alien world beyond."

Everyone gasps with amazement.

"Last week, your teacher asked you to prepare a presentation about your interest in land exploration," Dr. Lamprey continues. "What your teacher didn't tell you is that we are going to be judging those presentations and the winning student will get to train with Buzz to become a terranaut—with the possibility of accompanying him on his next mission!"

"That's if you *want* to accompany me," Buzz adds.

"Yes," Dr. Lamprey says. "Can we please have a show of fins from all those who would like to be considered."

All of us put a fin up.

Except Joe. His rear toots so loud this time, he becomes the first schoolkid ever to volunteer to be a terranaut by the power of his butt alone.

A hush has fallen over the gym. Just the mild rustle of seaweed in the current can be heard.

Mrs. Shelby has taken a seat next to Dr. Lamprey and Buzz Sharkfin. They are all waiting to judge our presentations.

Of course Rick has decided that he's

going to go first, and floats past, deliberately bumping into me. I'm sent spinning into Joe. "That's just for starters," Rick hisses.

Rick swims up to the stage.

"On you go, son," says Buzz, looking expectantly at Rick.

The whole school holds its gills.

"Every time I go on vacation to Finsney World, I ask Mom and Dad to take a detour to the John F. Kelpy Sea-Space Center," Rick begins. "The rides at Finsney World are okay, but what I really want to see are the terraships and to learn about the terranauts like Buzz!"

26

What a bunch of seaweed, I think.

Buzz nods, smiles, and fins to the crowd.

"I love seeing where they manage the expeditions at Fishon Control, and it's really great being able to buy all your official merchandise in the NASA store, Buzz."

More smiles from Buzz.

"I would be wearing my Buzz Sharkfin T-shirt now, but someone"—Rick drills his eyes into me like the dentist of doom—"ruined it!"

"Don't worry, son," says Buzz. "We'll get you a dozen new ones for you and your family."

I don't believe it!

"And to finish, all I want to say is that when I look up at the glinting waves overhead, and think of the endless sky and the distant lands, all I want to do is reach for the starfish and conquer sea-space for all oceankind!"

WHAAAAAAAAAAAAAAAAAT?????

I look in my schoolbag.

My presentation, the one I had been working on FOR AN ENTIRE WEEK, is missing! I see Rick stuffing a bit of crumpled paper into the pocket of his leather jacket. He must have stolen the last, and best, lines of my presentation when he bumped into me!

Everyone in the hall is going crazy. Buzz, Mrs. Shelby, and Dr. Lamprey are clapping as fast as their fins and flippers can manage!

Arrrrrrrrrrrrrrrrrrrrrrrrrrrrrrrrrrrgh!!!!!

Rick swims offstage and winks at

29

me. "Ha! I told you I'd get you back, Rubberhead. You're not going any-where near Buzz's Rocket."

I'm in such a panic I don't hear much of anybody else's presentation—I'm too busy trying to rewrite mine in my head. It's only when I hear Joe yelling, "No! Stop! It was all a mistake caused by my butt!" as Mrs. Shelby pushes him onto the stage, that my attention comes back to the hall. There's a stunned silence as Joe

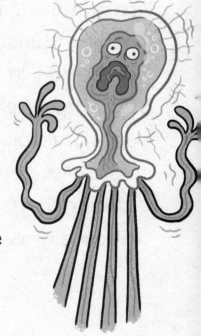

screams in Buzz's face, "Don't take me into space, you terranaughty shark! I DON'T WANT TO GO!!!" And then swims away as fast as he can.

I can't think of anything for my speech. And to make it *double worse*, the whispering around the hall is that Rick's was the best presentation EVER!

And it was. BECAUSE I WROTE IT.

"So, last but not least," announces Mrs. Shelby. "It's Harry Hammer!"

As I make my way to the stage, I can hear Rick snickering to his friend Donny Dogfish. "Here he comes! Space dork number one."

I look out at the sea of faces, and I can tell they think I won't be anywhere near as good as Rick.

I look at Buzz, who gives me a bored nod.

Mrs. Shelby gives me the tiniest of smiles.

Dr. Lamprey looks at her watch.

ZZZZZZZZZZZZING!!!!!!!!!!!!!!!!!!!

Just then, something stings me on my rear fin!

OWWWWWWWWWWWWWWW!!!!

I leap up into the school currents with a roar, trying to escape the pain.

ARRRRRRRRRRRRRRRRGHHHHH!!!

I spin up through the water, end over ending, turning, twisting, double-barrel rolling, fin-slapping, double-nose endy-ing, gill-sliding, and dorsal-diving—but the pain will not go away!

OWWWWWWWWWWWW!!!!!!!!!!!!!!!!!!

I shoot up blindly, trying to escape the sting in my butt, skimming the lobster-basketball

hoop, dipping in and out of the seawall bars.

What is stinging me?

I tail-kick and kick and kick, thinking there must be something attached to me, a stingray or a Portuguese man-o'-war, that I need to scrape off with the rush of speeding water. . . .

BUT NOTHING IS WORKING!!!!

I nose-wake back down toward the schoolkids—shooting a left-wheeling hammer-crisscross and a triple tail-over-hook, skidding to a halt next to Joe.

"I wondered where I'd left that," says Joe, pulling something from my underside.

Stuck to my backside was Joe's

spare venom sac! Youch! How did that ever happen? Luckily, now that Joe has plucked it off, the pain is receding.

Everyone, including Buzz, is looking at me.

I hang my hammer head in shame. Not only have I had my speech stolen by Rick, but I've made a complete fool of myself in front of the whole school and the ocean's greatest terranaut.

But . . .

Buzz sits up and starts to clap his fins together.

"Son, that was the most amazing set of aquabatics I have ever seen!"

Huh?????????

"You may not know this, but most terranauts start out as ace pilots pulling off just the kind of moves you did there. I've been completely knocked out by your skills!"

I cannot believe what I'm hearing!

"So, I can confidently say that there are TWO winners here today. The best two potential terranauts in Shark Point are Rick and Harry!" Buzz announces. "Both of you will travel with me to NASA headquarters to train as terranauts!"

Me, a terranaut!

CHAPTER 3

"FIVE!!!"

Dr. Lamprey's voice is tinny and metallic as she starts the countdown.

"FOUR!!"

I can see Buzz high up in the laboratory above the Landfall Test Pit.

"THREE!!"

The terrasuit I'm wearing feels so weird. Not only is the hammer-shaped helmet itchy around my neck, but the water tastes stale and fake. Yuck.

"TWO!!"

In front of me, the door into the main test pit starts to clank open on huge whale-bone hinges. I feel tiny. And more than a little scared.

"ONE!!"

That's when Rick barges past, pushing a sharp fin into my side and whirring the wheels on his space buggy, and zooms out into the sunlight!

"TEST BEGINS!!!!!!!!!!!!!!!!!!!!!!!!!!!"

I end up falling off my buggy with my butt in the air, and Rick rolls out into the Landfall Test Pit first, waving to Buzz as he goes.

Rick turns around—we need the vehicles or else we won't be able to move around outside the safe waters of the terraship—and comes back, holding out a fin to help me up.

I'm immediately suspicious. Why would he help me?

"Well done, Rick," booms Buzz over the loudspeakers in my hammer-shaped helmet. "We never leave a buddy behind."

Now I understand.

Rick only knocked me off so he could come back to help me up.

More showing off for Buzz.

I can't refuse the help, so I take hold and let Rick pull me back onto the buggy.

"Is that you impressing Buzz again?" I whisper to Rick.

Rick just gives me the sharkiest of grins and zooms off into the test area, leaving me in a cloud of dry dust!

So, here's my journal of everything that happened to get me here—yet again being made to look like stinky seaweed by Rick in front of Buzz.

My Terra-Training Journal, by Harry Hammer, Trainee Terranaut AND RUBBERHEADED GOOFBALL!!!

(Sorry, looks like Rick wrote that on my journal last night while I was on the phone with Mom. I'll get an eraser and remove it while you read.)

Day 1

Arrive at John F. Kelp SeaSpace Center for training.

Rick has already nabbed the top bunk in our rooms.

Great.

Feeling a very long way from home, but spoke to Dad on the phone. He just wanted to talk about his latest speech and how fantastic he is as mayor. That made me want to go home a lot less. Tomorrow my training to be a terranaut starts in the SeaSpace Lab. Can't wait.

Day 2

Got fitted with my terrasuit today.

Well . . . when I say I got fitted, I got fitted with most of it. All except the helmet. Because my helmet has to be built in the shape of a hammer, it takes much longer to make, so it isn't ready yet. I've got to wait.

Rick's is ready and he's spent all day getting used to it.

He's already gone into the Landfall Test Pit (big box of dry land where they've sucked out all the water so we can experience being terranauts.

Rick is going to be days ahead of me, because of MY RIDICULOUS HAMMERY HEAD. ☹

Day 25

Wow!

Just finished three weeks of math and science.

It seems being a terranaut isn't all spinning around looking cool and sticking flags in stuff.

Some of the problems made Rick's eyes
go funny. He's not the sharpest tooth in the
jaw. Buzz was really impressed with me. But
Rick wasn't when I laughed at him all the
way back to our room!

Day 29

I just swam hammer-first into a wall.

Dr. Lamprey had me climb onto the legs
of an octopus named Nigel, who spun me
around so fast (to test how my body reacts
to increased gravity and high speeds) that
my eyes went as googly and as crossed as
Rick's had during the science classes.

And let me tell you, when a hammerhead
goes cross-eyed, he looks like he's tied a
knot in his face.

It. Is. Not. Pretty.

I knew I shouldn't have laughed at Rick

after the math test. He's laughing at me now as I keep swimming into things, and he's taking pictures for Plaicebook and Finstagram.

Grump.

Day 40

Rick is getting on my nerves. All he tries to do every day is make Buzz think he's the best at stuff.

I mean, yeah, he's stronger than me. But that's because he's a reef shark, and reef sharks are really strong, so that's not my fault, is it?

He's also faster than me, and that's again because he's a reef shark, and reef sharks are really fast. . . .

He's just better than me, isn't he? ☹

Everything rests on tomorrow.

Tomorrow is the last day of training and we're going to be testing out new buggies in the Landfall Test Pit. This is going to be the final chance to show who the best is. Little does Rick know I've been practicing on mine every night for an extra hour while he snores on his top bunk!

I'm going to beat him for sure!

So, yeah. Things don't quite turn out how I plan. Rick pushes me off the buggy, comes back to help me up, and then leaves me in a cloud of dust, making him look so much better than me all over again.

When will I ever learn???????

The dust in the Test Pit begins to settle.

Rick is already off and zooming over

the pretend sand dunes, around the plastic palm trees, and under a few odd-looking rock formations copied from photographs from previous unsharked sea-probe missions. Rick is driving his cart like a pro, leaving me trying to kick-start the engine on mine.

Just as I get the engine roaring into life, Dr. Lamprey blows the horn to signal the end of the mission and speaks into her microphone.

"Well done, boys," she says. "We'll end it there! You've both been great!"

"Both?" says Rick. "Harry didn't even get his buggy going!"

I look at Rick. Here we go again.

Buzz, now in his own terrasuit, drops down into the Test Pit with a big smile on his face. "No he didn't, Rick, but what he did do was not panic, or lose focus."

I didn't?

"Harry knew that what was important was not getting upset, but to stay calm and work hard to get his vehicle going. That's just the sort of terranaut we need. You're each as good as the other, but in very different ways. You with your brawn, Rick, and you, Harry, with your brains."

Wow.

"Together, you're the perfect team.

And because of that we've decided that you'll both accompany me on my next mission."

This time Rick doesn't need to knock me over. I fall backward with glee, kicking my terrasuited tail in the air with joy!

Day 50

Mission Day!

A huge crowd has gathered around the John F. Kelpy SeaSpace Center to see us off. I can see them out of the corner of my hammer on the screen above my head, but I really don't want to look.

I'm writing this quickly, as I'm currently getting strapped into the terraship command module at the top of our rocket, *Apollock 11*.

Buzz is in the center seat, and Rick and I are on either side as we go through our pre-flight checks.

Luckily, we don't have to have our helmets on yet, as the *Apollock 11* is filled with lovely fresh seawater circulated by pumps deep in the midsection of the rocket.

Rick is sucking on a tube of Kelp Paste and looks just as nervous as I feel.

Buzz of course is very calm as he fins switches and talks to the NASA clammander in the Fishon Control Tower.

What?

Why don't I want to look at the screen?

Simple.

My dad is about to make a speech about me, and my mom is floating beside him wearing a T-shirt plastered with the words HARRY WARRY on the front and MY SHOOTING STARFISH on the back.

They keep showing it on the TV coverage and I just want to curl up and disappear.

"Can't we turn the sound off?" I ask Buzz as he turns dials and sets navigation data into the control panel above us.

"Don't you want to hear your dad make his speech, son?" asks Buzz.

"Have you ever met my dad, Buzz?"

"Nope, but he looks like a fine shark. You should be proud to be his son."

"I am," I say. "Right up until he starts speaking. You'll see."

On the screen, Dad floats up to the TV lobster's microphone and addresses the entire crowd. "Thank you all for coming here today to see me."

I look at Buzz.

Buzz looks at me.

"I have generously consented to let my son, Harry Hammer, travel with Mr. Bozz Shirtdorsal on the *Appalling 11* to a strange alien world today. . . . I guess you're all wondering how I feel about that . . . well . . ."

Buzz looks at me.

I look at Buzz.

Buzz turns the sound off on the screen. "I see what you mean," he says, patting me sympathetically on the hammer.

"He's all right," I say. "Mostly."

Buzz grins and settles down.

"Well, boys, here we go. . . ."

I look at Rick.

Rick is cross-eyed with fear. He puts his fins over his face. "Maybe it wasn't such a good idea to steal Harry's speech after all." I hear him whispering.

The clammander in Fishon Control says, "All checks complete. *Apollock 11* is ready for splashoff!!"

Gulp!

"START THE COUNTDOWN!!!!!!"

Earth, here we come!

CHAPTER 4

"FIVE!!!"

Rick yells "Mommy!" and reaches for Buzz's fin!

"FOUR!!"

I think *Mommy!* and reach for Buzz's other fin!

"THREE!!!"

"Hold tight, boys!" yells Buzz as the engines beneath *Apollock 11* rumble to life, and the whole ocean seems to shake around us! "TWO!!!!!!!!!!!!!!!!!!!!!!!!!!!!!!!!!!!!!!!"

"Arrrrrrrrgh!" Rick and I both yell, as clouds of orange flames fill the portholes.

"ONE!!"

"Go for main engine start," says the clammander in Fishon Control.

"SPLASHUP!!"

"*Apollock 11*, oceankind's most ambitious mission yet to land on land, is clearing the tower. Everything looks good!"

No it doesn't! Nothing looks good.

My teeth are rattling, my eyes can't focus, and my head is being FLUBBBBBBERRREDDDDDDD by the sea force!

I look around at Buzz and Rick.

I see their faces are being as bent and rippled by the force of the splashoff as mine.

"*Apollock 11* has reached seascape velocity and will be breaking through the overhead waves in . . . three . . . two . . . one . . . and BREAKTHROUGH!!!!"

A burst of hot sunlight comes through the porthole, illuminating the module with intense rays.

"Helmets on!" shouts Buzz. "We're clear of the ocean now."

I fumble around for my hammer-shaped helmet as the waves of the ocean drop away faster and faster through the porthole.

Up above, the sky is deep blue, and in the distance I can just make out the mountains and beaches of land!

"Changing to horizontal flight," Buzz says, operating a control and steering the rocket to the flatter flight path.

"I wanna go home," whispers Rick.

It's all I can do not to agree with him. The ocean looks a very long way away now.

We zoom on toward land, bursting through clouds, hearing the rush of wind on the outside of the module. Strange white flying things, with orange pointy noses and flappy, feathery side fins, circle in the distance. I don't know what they are, but they seem pretty interested in us.

"Hey, Harry," says Buzz, looking at the creatures too. "Write down and describe any alien life-forms we see. It's important we take back as much information as possible."

"Okay, Buzz," I say, getting out my lily pad. I'm glad to have something to do to distract me from the incredible speed of the rocket.

CREATURE ONE—The Flying Orange Nose Fin Flapper Thing
(I know it's not a great name, but right now, it's the best I've got.) It flies.

It's got an orange nose and odd-shaped fins for flying.

I hope I get better at spotting these alien life-forms.

Soon the ocean is a distant memory and *Apollock 11* is completely over land!

I've never been so far from the sea before. I look down at the mountains below. They look so weird not covered in water. Almost in a flash the mountains are gone, and we're out over a really flat plane. Rick has recovered from his land panic and is looking down. "What's that?" he says, pointing at a—

CREATURE TWO—A Red Square Thing on Black Wheels Digging Up a Field

This is a really weird animal. I only get a second to see it, but it appears to be a creature that puts straight lines in mud in weird-looking fields, while blowing dark gray smoke out of a whale-like breathing tube to the side of its face. I wonder what it does?

Buzz is pulling back on the throttle, and *Apollock 11* begins to slow down. Up ahead I see a wide expanse of land-scape with some weird-looking seaweed laid out in long straight lines.

This whole place is so *alien*.

Buzz brings the *Apollock 11* back to vertical and prepares to descend to land.

"Touchdown!" Buzz says into the radio . . . but all that comes back is a hiss.

"What's the matter?" I ask.

"We've lost contact with the guys at Fishon Control, but don't worry, it's probably all the shaking from splashoff. I'll have it fixed as soon as I can."

I look at Rick.

Rick looks at me.

Gulp!

"Right!" yells Buzz, undoing his safety belt. "Let's get this party started!"

Now that we've landed, Rick is feeling much braver. He's stopped asking for his "Mommy" and is again pushing me out of the way to get off the command deck of *Apollock 11* and into the hold where the buggies are stored.

"Hey!" I shout at Rick as he shoves me away.

Buzz laughs.

"That's what I like to see, real enthusiasm!"

What I'd like to see is Rick drive right into a deep, dark hole!

Soon, the three of us are in our buggies and are waiting with bated breath for the door in the side of the module to open and the ramp to descend. All I can hear in my helmet as Buzz operates the control to drain the water and open the ship is my own breathing—loud and raspy in my ears. I sound just like the villain from that movie *Starfish Wars*—you know, the horrible black shark with the flowing cloak and terrifying mask . . . Darth Wader.

Anyway, while I've been thinking about that, all the water has drained from the module and the door is clanking open, letting in sunlight.

The ramp *wzzzzzzzzzzzzzzzzzed* down and Buzz raises his fin into the air. "Okay, boys, let's do it!"

My heart is bouncing around my rib cage like a fat tuna trapped in a cave. My hammer eyes squint in the sunlight as our vehicles clear the *Apollock 11* fuselage and start to roll down the ramp toward the ground.

"Ready?" Buzz steers off the ramp and onto the dusty earth. Rick zooms ahead of me and skids up a cloud of dirt that completely fogs my vision. I'm still wiping the dust off my visor as Rick and Buzz lean over the side of their buggies to put their finprints down!

"That's three . . . no . . . TWO . . . small finprints for shark. And LOADS of

giant shark history for all OCEANKIND!"
says Buzz into his radio log.

Through the smears of mud and dust,
I can just see Rick and Buzz high-fin-
ning. I finally manage to clank off the
ramp and make my own finprint. "That's
one tiny finprint for a hammerhead, and
not much else for oceankind," I whisper
to myself.

Rick has beaten me again.

"Okay, terranauts," says Buzz. "I'm going to stay here to try to fix the communication gear. I want you to go off on your own, not too far, and collect some samples of local geology and plant life. Harry, I want you to keep making notes on any alien creature you come across. Okay?"

Rick and I salute Buzz, although I manage to smear even more dust over my visor as I do so.

Rick's terrasuit is spotless. My terrasuit looks like I'd been rolling in low-tide mud on the Shark Point shallows. Buzz wipes my visor with a sponge he pulls from a pocket in his terrasuit.

"You need to look after this terrasuit, son—it's keeping you alive. Remember that."

As I nod up at the famous terranaut, I swear I can hear Rick snickering as Buzz wipes me clean *exactly* like my mom does with her hanky at the school gates.

Grump.

I'm supposed to be enjoying this adventure of a lifetime, and Rick is determined to spoil it!

We've driven the buggies about a thousand miles from the *Apollock 11*. I'm quickly writing reports of the alien creatures I've found.

CREATURE THREE—
The Two-Horned
Moo-Monster
These weird
ones live in herds,
make really odd "mooing" noises, and
manufacture sticky brown hats from
their back ends.

CREATURE FOUR—The Hairy-Yappy-Fur
Waggle-Tail
This one burst out of a hedge and just
sat there yapping at us. It was wearing a
collar with a little silver disc hanging off it. I

couldn't read the word it said on the disc because it was in a weird alien language, but I'll copy it out here: TOTO.

I ask Rick if he thinks the Yappy-Fur is trying to warn us of danger, but Rick just shrugs. "Who cares?"

Rick's having more fun skidding his buggy around in the dust while I do all the work. *DOUBLE GRUMP.*

CREATURE FIVE—The Long-Faced-Hoofed Skitter

This one stuck its long nose over a hedge.

71

said something that sounded like *"Neigh"* and ran away as Rick tried to grab the long hairs on the top of its neck.

"We're not supposed to catch them, Rick!" I shout.

Rick just fins his nose at me and speeds away, saying, "You can follow the rules all you like! I'm gonna have me some fun!"

At that moment the Yappy-Fur races up to us again, going absolutely crazy! It runs up and down in front of us, yapping for all it's worth. It jumps up and down on the spot, wagging its tail and getting all the more frustrated.

PING!

PING! *PING!* PING! *PING!*

Suddenly the emergency activation on my hammer-vision kicks in and my visor is filled with a rush of information from my hammer-head warning/sonar system. Hammerheads may have the silliest shaped heads in the ocean, but with hammer-vision, we have some of the coolest and most advanced warning senses *EVER*.

My hammer-vision is telling me something's approaching from the northeast, and it's approaching fast!

It would be with us in . . .

TEN SECONDS!!!

What *is* it?

NINE SECONDS!!

My hammer-vision's telling me nothing. . . .

EIGHT SECONDS!!!

Except *SOMETHING* is coming!!!

SEVEN SECONDS!!

I can hear a rumbling, like a sudden storm, or the huge propeller on a leggy airbreather's ocean-going liner. But this is bigger. Much bigger.

SIX SECONDS!!

I switch off my hammer-vision and scan the sky.

O.M.C.!!!!!!!!

The air is turning black around us. Rick is staring up with his mouth open. The Yappy-Fur is going even crazier!!!!!

There is a *WHIRLPOOL* in the air, but instead of being made of water, this one is made of wind and is tearing up the ground, the hedges, the dirt, and the alien creatures we have seen.

It's a *TORNADO*!!!!!

I see a Moo-Monster spin off its feet and spiral high up into the column of air. This moving, twisting, terrifying air pool of destruction that's going to rip through Rick, me, and the Yappy-Fur in . . .

CHAPTER 5

"FIVE SECONDS!!"

"Rick, we have to get back to the ship!"

"FOUR SECONDS!!!"

Rick and I turn our buggies around as the Yappy-Fur leaps up onto my tail and hangs on with his sharp little teeth!

"THREE SECONDS!!!!!!!!!!!!!!!!!!!!!!!!!!!!!!!!!!!!"

I hope he doesn't puncture my terrasuit, but I can't leave him here to get swallowed up like the Moo-Monster!!!!

"TWO SECONDS!!!!!!!!!!!!!!!!!!!!!!!!!!!!!!!!!!!!!"

We race off!!!

"ONE SECOND!!"

The rumble of the tornado is catching us. We're not going to make it! It's going to . . .

LIFT us OFF the ground!!!!!!!!!!!!!!!!!!!!!!!!!!!!

WHHHHHHOOOOOSSSSSSHHH!!!!

And we're up, off and spinning into the air, whirling around, out of control, and completely out of luck!!!!

Arrrrrrrrrrrrrrrrrrrghghghghg!!!!!!!!!!

Dark.

I open my eyes.

Still dark.

I can't hear the tornado anymore. That's a good thing.

I can't see. That's not a good thing.

I use my fins to check that the terra-suit is okay.

The water is still in it and I can still breathe. That's a good thing.

But I can't move my tail or turn my head. I'm trapped under something heavy. That's a bad thing.

"H . . . H . . . Harry?" I hear Rick in my helmet radio. At least the communicator is still working. That's a good thing.

"Where are you, Harry?"

"I'm here!"

"Where's here?"

"I don't know."

"Neither do I."

"Yap! Yap! Yap!"

The Yappy-Fur is obviously close by, but I can't see it.

I feel something jump up onto my chest.

"Yap! Yap! Yap!"

It walks around on my terrasuit, and there's a *clink* as teeth bite into something.

"Yamph! Yamph! Yamph!"

WHAM!!!!

Suddenly my eyes can't cope with all the light that's flooding in!

The Yappy-Fur has pulled a piece of twisted coral off my helmet. Through the blinking and the squinting I can see I'm trapped under my wrecked buggy. It's been completely destroyed by the tornado, and the Yappy-Fur is trying to dig me out from under it.

Rick's buggy is about two miles away, upside down but intact. Rick's hanging by the seat belt, but he can't see me because his helmet is covered in Moo-Monster hats blown there while we were being spun around in the air pool.

"I can see you, Rick!"

The Yappy-Fur is dragging a seat off

my tail, and now I can move. I use my fins to begin to drag myself out of the pile of wreckage. By pushing with my tail, and using my hammer to hook into ridges in the ground, I can make good, if slow, progress.

Eventually I get to Rick, and I begin to use my tail to rock it backward and forward.

"What are you doing, you goon?!" yells Rick, his voice terrified and his fins flapping around trying to find something to hold on to.

"Just be quiet, Rick! I'm trying to help!"

With one final heave I push the buggy over and Rick is upright. The Yappy-Fur jumps up and down and does a spinny little dance to show how happy he is.

I start wiping some of the Moo-Monster hats from Rick's helmet.

"W-where . . . are we?" Rick says.

I look around. "I have no idea."

We seem to have landed between two huge box-like structures. Both have strange symbols on the front, like the ones on the Yappy-Fur's collar.

I can't read the symbols, but one has a huge yellow sign in a shape like this: M. And the other one has a white sea

apple with a chunk bitten out of the side.

I crane my neck to look in through a window.

The M structure has loads of tables and chairs blown over by the tornado, and there's thousands of what look like mini Moo-Monster hats all over the floor.

I have no idea what they could be.

I look in the Sea-Apple-with-a-Chunk-Bitten-Out's window.

This place is just as much of a mess. There're tons of smashed stuff all over the floor and everything is white. Little white boxes, big white boxes, medium-size white things, and other white stuff. Again.

No idea what's going on there, but they could do with adding a bit of color.

"Toto! You found him! Come here, boy!"

Arrrrrrrrrrrrrrrrrrrrrrrrrrghghghghghgh!!!!!

Rick and I jump in our terrasuits and spin around.

In front of us is the last thing I expected—or wanted—to see.

A leggy airbreather!!!!!

I'm completely confused. Why would there be one here, in this alien world? I thought the leggy airbreathers just lived on floaty boats or near the beaches of the oceans.

This leggy airbreather is no taller than me, has big glasses, lots of red hair, freckles on his nose, and is wearing a T-Shirt with a rocket on the front. The Yappy-Fur jumps up at the leggy airbreather and licks his face all over, obviously pleased to see him. The leggy airbreather's eyes suddenly widen when he realizes what he's looking at.

We look at him. Terrified.

All our lives we've been told to keep away from leggy airbreathers because they take us from the ocean with hooks and nets and turn us into dinner.

"Swim!" screams Rick.

"How?" I scream back.

"Coooooooooooooooooool car!" says the leggy airbreather.

Rick and I freeze.

The leggy airbreather comes up to us. "Thanks for finding my dog. When the tornado hit I thought I'd lost him forever. Also, radical buggy, dudes. I love your spacesuits, too. Are you, like, aliens?"

"Ummm," says Rick.

"Ummmmm," I say. Amazingly, I can understand his language.

"'Cause if you are aliens, guys, you'd better get out of town pretty fast. All the adults went to their shelters when the warning sounded, and they'll be out very soon. And once the government realizes there are aliens in town, they're gonna wanna capture you and do experiments on you or take you to Area 51 or something."

"How do you know?" I ask.

"I watch a lot of science fiction movies."

"Aren't you scared of us?" I say. "If we're aliens?"

"Nah," says the leggy airbreather. "If the movies I watch are true, then you're really the good guys just trying to get back to your spaceships, and have come in peace. You have come in peace, right?" The leggy airbreather pushes his glasses back up his nose and begins chewing on what looks like a fish sandwich.

"Yes," I say, nodding so hard I bang my head on the inside of my helmet.

"So," he says. "Where's your rocket?"

"Ummmmm," I say.

"Ummmmmmmmmmmm," says Rick.

The leggy airbreather looks serious. "Then, guys. We have a problem."

*BE-BOR! BE-BOR! WHOOP, WHOOP,
WHOOP!!!*

We look around wildly.

"What's that?!?!??" Rick asks.

"It's good news; it's just the cops letting everyone know it's safe to come out
of the tornado shelters."

"What in the world . . . ," a voice bellows from behind us, "is that?"

"Actually, it's bad news," says the
leggy airbreather.

The three of us spin around.

Blocking one exit between the build-
ings are two leggy airbreathers in blue
uniforms. They have mirrored glasses

91

over their eyes, and they're both wearing sea cowboy hats.

"What is that?" says one of them.

The leggy airbreather reaches between Rick and me and yanks the starting control for the buggy. The engine roars to life. "Go!" he shouts.

"Which way?" I scream.

"Any way!" he shouts.

"YAP! YAP! YAP!"

The Yappy-Fur starts running away, then stops, spins, and runs away again.

"Follow the dog!" yells the leggy air-breather.

Rick hits the accelerator and I hang on for dear life as we shoot off. The buggy is really only made for one shark, so I have to squeeze myself in down by Rick's tail, grip tight to his dorsal, and stick my hammer in his finpit.

ZOOOOOOOOOOOOOOOOOOOM!!!!!!!!!!!

I look back to see that the leggy air-breather has tripped up one of the ones in a sea cowboy hat, and is blocking the other one with his legs.

"Faster!!!!" I yell.

"I am!!!" shouts Rick. "And get your head out of my finpit. It t-t-t-t-tickles!"

Rick starts laughing uncontrollably and the cart veers off to the left.

We just about miss a wall, and then burst out into clear air.

All around us the leggy airbreather town is coming to life.

There are metal boxes on wheels zooming around the place. There are leggy airbreathers starting to pick up the mess caused by the raging tornado. And there are others just looking happy that they're okay.

Luckily, not many of them are taking much notice of us as we roar past.

"Hey, wait for me!"

I look behind to see that the leggy airbreather who helped us is peddling furiously on his own set of wheels, trying to catch up. In the far distance the sea cowboys are running after us too, puffing hard, nearly out of breath.

"I'm Elliot," the leggy airbreather says, shaking my fin.

"I'm Harry," I say. "And this is Rick."

"Glad to meet you," says Elliot, peddling his feet in a blur, "but we aren't going to be safe for long."

Oh. That sounds bad. "Why?"

"I have a bad feeling about this."

Elliot points way back in the distance. The sea cowboys, or "cops" as he calls them, are climbing into a huge yellow metal box on wheels. There are windows all down the side of it, and at the windows we can see the faces of lots of leggy airbreathers the same size as Elliot.

"They've commandeered the SCHOOL BUS!!!!" shouts Elliot. "DRIVE!!!!!!!!!!!!!!!!!!!!!!!!"

Rick presses his fin down on the accelerator and we go top speed!

Things get a little complicated at this point, but I'll list what happens the best I can . . .

We zoom out of town, following the Yappy-Fur.

The school bus chugs after us, with the cops
   driving as hard as they can.

We fly across a bridge, with the metal boxes, or "cars"
   as Elliot calls them, having to skid out of the way.

We head for the hills.

The bus starts gaining on us!

We drive into a gloomy place that Elliot calls
   the "woods." They look exactly like a spooky
   seaweed forest.

Elliot tells us to hide behind a tree.

The bus *whizzes* past.

We go in the opposite direction! The Yappy-Fur
   jumps up onto the vehicle and points with his
   nose in the direction we should go.

98

We burst out of the woods, and there's the
    school bus parked across the road—waiting
    for us. Our trick didn't work!!!!
I grab the controls from Rick and ram my tail
    down on the accelerator. I point the buggy up
    the slope next to the road, and as we blast
    above the treeline, we . . .

"ARRRRRRRRRRRRGHHHHHHH!!!!"
"OH NOOOOOOOOOOOOOOOOO!!!!"
"MOMMMMMMMMMMMMMMMMYYYY!!!!!"
"YAP! YAP! YAP! YAP! YAP! YAP! YAP!
YAP! YAP! YAP! YAP! YAP!"
Suddenly we're airborne!
YES!!! HIGH IN THE AIR!!!

99

HOW IS THIS HAPPENING???

There's no tornado, the buggy isn't equipped with a flying mechanism, and yet here we are. Soaring over the woods, the road, and the trees, and the school bus is disappearing below us as we go up, up, and away!!!!

I look at Elliot, who is still pedaling his bike. In midair!

I look at Rick. He has his eyes closed and is saying, "Mommymommymommy-mommy," under his breath.

I look at the Yappy-Fur. He's yapping at something behind me.

I turn.

I see it.

I can't believe my hammer!

"But . . . ," I say to myself, "that's IMPOSSIBLE!!!!!!!"

CHAPTER 6

"FIVE!!!"

Buzz's voice crackles to life in my helmet.

"FOUR!!!"

He shouts, "I need you to get ready, boys!

"THREE!!!"

"What's happening, Buzz???"

"TWO!!

"No time to tell you," he calls back. "Just hang on, it's going to be some ride!

"ONE!!

"Traction beam! Full POWER!!!!!

"HERE WE GO!!!"

Rick and I grab the flying buggy for dear life as Buzz flies the *Apollock 11* out from behind a cloud, swoops over us, opens the door in the side, and operates the traction beam to yank us all inside!

In a tangle of fins, arms, buggies, bikes, and Yappy-Fur, we lay in a heap in the hold as the rocket powers us away from danger.

We're saved!!!!!

"So after the tornado had blown past and I couldn't find you boys, I got on with fixing the controls," Buzz explains. "Once they were all up and running, I used the rocket's W.A.D.A.R. to locate you both and the buggies, flew to where you were, saw you were in trouble, then used the TRACTION beam to lift you up and into the hold!" Buzz is sitting back on his flight couch, looking very pleased with himself.

Elliot is openmouthed with wonder, looking at all the flight controls. "I've never been in an *Unidentified Fishy Object* before," he gasps. "But IT'S JUST LIKE THE MOVIES! Only with more . . . you know . . . sharks." Elliot shakes my fin. "Thank you! This is the best thing ever!"

Yappy-Fur is loving it too, jumping up and down and doing little somersaults.

"We'll drop you off back in town, and then we'll head for home," Buzz tells us, smiling.

Elliot's grin is so wide, you could probably swim a dolphin through it.

"Bye, Elliot!" I say as the young leggy airbreather walks back across the field we landed in. Yappy-Fur gives me a cuddle and licks my terrasuit all over.

"Bye, Harry," Elliot calls. "That was amazing!"

Buzz and I wave as the door closes in the side of the rocket. "Okay," says Buzz. "You two tidy up in here, and I'll get the preflight checks started."

Buzz presses a button on the wall and the compartment starts to fill with water. I can't wait for it to reach the ceiling. I am desperate to get out of my terrasuit and have a swim. My skin itches like crazy.

"Hey, Rick, it'll be great to get back to Shark Point, won't it?" I say as the water goes up past my hammer.

Rick has been strangely quiet for ages. As I watch him now, his eyes are downcast and he's just looking at his tail, not making any attempt to take off his terrasuit.

"What's up?" I ask him.

Rick says nothing.

"Come on," I say. "We've just had the adventure of a lifetime. Why are you so sad?"

"Wouldn't you be?" he says.

"Why?"

"You're going back a hero. I'm going back as the shark who shouted 'Mommy' four hundred times whenever there was danger. I'm worse than that butt-tooting Joe the Jellyfish!"

I'm confused.

"How will they find out?" I ask.

Rick locks eyes with me from inside his helmet. "Because I've always been horrible to you, and I bet you can't wait to get back to tell everyone what a coward I am."

With that, Rick turns around and floats up to the cockpit, slamming the door hard behind him.

"And as I'm sure you're all aware, it was my only son, Harry, whom I bravely let travel with Buzz Sharkfin."

As usual, Dad is hogging the limelight. We've landed back at the John F. Kelpy SeaSpace Center—Buzz had flown us in perfectly.

It had been a strange journey, with me writing up all my alien reports, and Rick refusing to speak to me, however many times I tried.

We float out of the *Apollock 11* to a full hero's welcome. Thousands of

oceankind have gathered at the landing pad, watching us descend from the high, sparkly waves above, down into the safe, gloomy depths of the sea.

Mom is the first to greet me in a flurry of kisses and fins. Luckily, I'm still wearing my hammer helmet so she can't plant yucky, sloppy kisses all over me. But I do want to throw up when she calls me her "Little Spangly Starfish!"

And just to make things worse, Dad has gotten himself in front of the cameras and is pretty much interviewing himself.

Buzz raises a fin, and the crowd come to a hush. "Friends and relatives,

we are home." His voice booms around the landing pad. "We had the pleasure of discovering a wealth of alien creatures and have brought back many pictures and samples of a world you can scarcely believe exists."

The TV news crew lobsters rush up to us, eager for an interview. All microphones pointing at Buzz.

Buzz shakes his head.

"No! No! These boy sharks are the real heroes! Why don't you interview them first? They had a much wilder adventure than me—they got caught up in a tornado!"

The crowd gasps as the lobsters point their microphones at Rick.

I can see Rick doesn't know what to do. His face is turning red, and if I'm not mistaken, he looks like he's about to burst into tears.

I reach out a fin and shake with Rick,

then with the other fin, I pull the microphone to my mouth.

"Let me tell you," I begin. Rick looks
up at me, his eyes red and his bottom
lip quivering. "Let me tell you about Rick
Reef—the bravest shark I know and the
one who saved me from the tornado,
the leggy airbreathers, and the massive
Moo-Monster!"

Later, at a party arranged by NASA, Joe
and Tony are seeing who can eat the wid-
est sea cucumber sideways, and Ralph,
my pilot fish pal, is enjoying darting in and

out of my mouth, picking out the bits and pieces of party food stuck in my teeth.

As Ralph comes out of my mouth for about the hundredth time, with the most satisfied grin on his face I have ever seen, I feel a tugging on my fin.

It's Rick.

"I can't believe what you said."

"I can," I said. "We were both just as scared. And you were just as brave as me."

"Yeah, but you didn't call out for your mommy."

"I did," I said. "I just did it inside my head. Look, Rick, I know we don't get along and stuff, but you drove that buggy away from the cops, and you kept driving no matter what. Neither of us would be here today if it wasn't for you. I'm not going to tell tales about you."

Rick looks on the verge of tears again. He holds out his fin.

I take hold of it, and we shake fins like buddies.

I don't guess we'll ever be *best buddies*. And I'm sure he'll still FLUBBER me whenever he gets a chance, but I do feel things between us will be a lot better from now on.

And that feeling makes all the danger worthwhile.

"Five!!"

Dad yells as the anglerfish candles light up on top of the celebration cake NASA has provided.

"Four!!"

Dad shouts as me, Buzz, and Rick swim forward.

"Three!!"

Dad booms as the three of us gill in a huge breath!

"Two!!"

Dad raises a NASA flag in his fin.

"One!!"

Dad brings the flag down with a mighty *SWOOSH!!!!!*

"SPLASHUP!!!"

Rick and I blow at the candles with our huge breaths, and one by one, the flames go out . . . like stars as the sun rises.

THE END